TOMBSTONES
Volume 1
Ant Farm

D0711770

13 Digit ISBN 978-1532956898
10 Digit ISBN 1532956894

Printed in the United States of America

The characters and events in this book are fictitious. Any similarity to real persons, living, dead, or undead is coincidental and not intended by the author.

Living in constant fear and loss of sleep is intended by the author.

Tombstonesbooks.com 2016

Ant Farm

Screamin Calhoun

Ant Farm

Screamin Calhoun

TOMBSTONES Volume 1
ANT FARM
Chapter 1

Great, this is gonna be a crappy birthday, Matt thought as he stepped out onto his front porch and prepared for yet another horrible day of school.

It was March fifteenth. The birds were singing, the sun was shining, and it was warm enough to wear shorts. This should have had all the makings of a perfect eleventh birthday, but not for Matt.

"Why couldn't my birthday be on a weekend?" he complained to no one in particular.

Celebrating his birthday at school wasn't his idea of a party. Matt wasn't one of the popular kids. But that didn't really bother him. He sort of preferred to hang out alone, anyway, but most kids thought he was weird for that. When the "cool" kids did speak to him, it was usually something like, "Hey, loser" or "What's up, DoorMatt?"

But Matt didn't hate school. He just hated *going* to school. He had to take the long way there so he could avoid the real problem: Jack Callahan, the neighborhood bully.

Walking through the woods was a death wish. Matt may as well have thrown his milk money away, given himself a noogie, and pulled his underwear over his head to save himself the time and Jack the energy.

So Matt would have to take the scenic routes. It was important to take different paths all the time. Every morning was spent in total fear, and it was exhausting. If he managed to avoid one of Jack's atomic wedgies, it only meant that there was one fewer thing that the other average jerks at school could tease him about for the next seven hours.

But they could always find something else to be mean about.

So with a knot in his stomach, Matt started off for school with the terrible feeling that this was going to be the worst birthday he ever had.

Lately, he had been walking down past the crossing guard and continuing four blocks to the right to avoid the woods and playground altogether. He had found an alley between the corner store and an old house that took a few blocks off the trip. Once he made it through the alley, he only needed to cross the grocery store parking lot before he would arrive at the front entrance to Lakemont Elementary School.

It had been almost a full week of avoiding Jack by following this route, and with every day came the growing sense that he was pressing his luck. But why change something that was working perfectly?

As Matt approached the corner store, he paused, staring at the entrance to the alley. He could continue down Main Street four more blocks and get to school just fine, but it would take an extra five minutes.

It was worth the risk. He would just have to go quickly.

He turned down the alley and tried to walk as fast as possible without looking scared. He wanted to remain completely invisible to anyone who might be around.

By the time Matt was halfway down the alley, his heart was pounding—not just from walking so fast, but also from the fear of being caught.

In front of him, on the right side of the alley, was a dumpster. Past the dumpster he could see cars in the grocery store parking lot. He suddenly thought he heard footsteps behind him. He turned and looked back over his shoulder.

Good, nothing there.

He turned to look forward and then, *BAM!*

He had smacked right into the side of the dumpster. He clunked his head and fell backwards with a thud. He let out a muffled groan of pain and lay on his back for a while, holding the side of his head.

After about five seconds, he took his hand away to see if his head were bleeding. It wasn't, but there was definitely a good lump developing.

What an idiot, he thought.

He looked back down the alley, expecting half the school to be standing there pointing and laughing. The alley was empty.

With a sigh of relief, he got back on his feet.

"Phew, no witnesses."

Matt picked up his backpack and felt the lump on his head once again. He rubbed it and thought how stupid it was going to look to all of his great friends at school.

It could have been worse, he thought. *At least my money and my underwear are still in place.*

As he shuffled around the dumpster, looking down and holding his head, he walked right into Jack. He had seen the whole thing.

ANT FARM

Chapter 2

"Good morning, freak. Have a nice trip?" Jack said, grabbing Matt by his shirt.

"Leave me alone," Matt said. He tried to squirm out of Jack's grasp, but Jack simply tightened his grip and slammed him against the same dumpster he had just run into.

"Oh, sure," Jack said. "I'll leave you alone just as soon as you pay your toll."

Matt swallowed hard and handed over his backpack.

"And I want that swell band on your wrist. Hand it over!"

Matt removed the tie-dyed rubber band bracelet that he had been wearing for the past week and gave it to Jack.

"Soooo, what's for lunch today, buddy?" Jack unzipped the backpack and took out the lunchbox. Inside was by far the best lunch his mom had packed for him all year. After all, it was his birthday.

Jack snatched the extra-large bag of chips and all of the homemade chocolate chip cookies. He then noticed the note inside. He took it out and read it aloud:

Matthew,

I hope everything is perfect for your special day. Happy Birthday. I love you,
Mom

"Put it back, Jack," Matt said with a scowl.

"Aw, your special day. Ya know, because this day is so special, I think I'll reduce your toll."

Jack took out one of the cookies, opened up the backpack, and proceeded to crumble it on top of all of the books.

"Happy birthday, freak!"

As he walked away, he picked up the backpack and threw it into the dumpster.

Matt did everything he could to fight back the tears. He could feel the pure anger rising up inside of him as he watched the jerk walk away. He wanted so badly to hurt him. If, for once, Jack could feel the humiliation and embarrassment of being pushed around.

Then something just clicked inside of him. He ran straight towards Jack, who was walking away munching on a cookie, chewing so loud that he didn't hear Matt coming.

Matt jumped in the air and planted his foot squarely in the middle of Jack's back.

Jack's head whipped backwards as he was knocked to the ground. The cookie went flying, and he landed hard on the dirty cement. His hands sort of broke his fall, but his face certainly took most of it.

Matt stood there, bewildered. If he hadn't been in complete shock, he would have been running for his life by now. But he was frozen. He couldn't believe what he had done and how good it felt. Like an erupting volcano, a rush of anger exploded into a furious release of action. It was a feeling of pure energy. He didn't feel afraid anymore, although logically he should have.

Jack scrambled to his feet, looking even more surprised than Matt did. He brushed off his hands on his jeans, which now had a gaping hole in the right knee.

He looked down at his hands and could see the dirt and gravel mixed with blood on both of them. Then he touched the right side of his face and looked at his hand once again...more blood.

"Aw, man, you're gonna pay for that," Jack said. "I'm gonna kill you, ya little weasel!"

Jack's voice woke Matt up. Once again, his body took over, but at least this time it decided to run. He dashed off as fast as he could, straight out of the alley and into the parking lot across from the school. Jack was right on his heels and gaining.

Matt ran like never before. He wasn't strong, but he was fast. Unfortunately, Jack was strong *and* fast.

Just before the end of the parking lot, Jack's hand grabbed the back of Matt's collar. He brought him to a sudden halt and nearly picked him off of the ground.

Matt knew he was about to pay for his moment in the sun.

Jack spun him around and punched him just below his left eye. Matt felt like he had been hit with a baseball bat. His ears were ringing, and he wasn't sure where he was.

He staggered backwards three or four steps with Jack charging towards him. As Jack cocked his fist for the next punishing blow, he was grabbed from behind by someone walking through the parking lot.

It was Mr. Evans, the very large gym teacher.

"Hey! Hey! Stop it! What's going on here?"

Mr. Evans looked at Matt and saw the lump quickly forming under his eye. Then he looked back at Jack, who looked much worse than Matt. He seemed confused about who was beating up whom. He had never seen Jack Callahan on the losing side of a fight and had to try hard to keep from smiling at this.

"All right, you're both coming with me to the principal's office." He grabbed them each by the arm and headed across the street to the school.

The boys struggled just to keep pace with Mr. Evans. As they were being dragged up the front steps with forty or fifty kids watching in amazement, Matt thought, *Maybe this wouldn't be the worst birthday after all.*

ANT FARM

Chapter 3

    Mr. Evans plopped both of them down in front of Mrs. West.

    Matt had never been to the principal's office. He doubted that Mrs. North even knew his name. After all, he was very forgettable.

    Matt was quiet, partially out of respect, but mostly out of fear. Jack sat there, oozing anger out of every pore of his skin. Mr. Evans stood between the two of them with one hand on the back of each of their chairs.

    "Well, what on earth has happened here?" Mrs. West asked.

    "I found the two of them fighting across the street," said Mr. Evans.

"Jack," Mrs. West turned towards him, "you seem to have become a regular visitor here. Why don't you start with your version of the events?"

"I was just minding my own business," he began, "when all of a sudden he just ran up and kicked me right in the back. He started it!"

"Well, that would be a first," Mrs. West said. She then turned toward Matt. "I'm sure you must have something to add to Mr. Callahan's story."

Matt told his version of the morning's events. His story was made that much more believable by the fact that Jack would interrupt every other sentence by blurting out something like, "He's a lying piece of dirt!"

But what really sealed Jack's fate was when he stood up and yelled, "You're dead meat, punk! I'm gonna kill you!" Mr. Evans had to hold him back from attacking Matt right in front of the principal.

They were taken to separate rooms to wait for their parents. Matt couldn't even get homework done because his book bag was still in the dumpster. Finally, after what seemed like a month, Matt was called back into Mrs. West's office, where his parents were waiting for him.

"Well, we've had quite a day," Mrs. West began. "As you can see, Matthew was involved in a fight with another boy off school grounds this morning. It appears that the other child started it, but that Matthew was responsible for the physical contact.

"This other child has already been suspended twice for fighting. And as a result, we are expelling him."

Matt's eyes became as wide as two quarters. He didn't know whether to be excited or terrified by this information.

Mrs. West continued, "We have a very strict policy about fighting, and there are no exceptions. There are other ways of dealing with a situation like this, and fighting is never acceptable. Matt needs to find other ways solve a problem, such as coming to a teacher. What all this means is that Matthew will serve a one-day suspension immediately."

His dad flashed him a stern glance and then winked at him, smiling at the corner of his mouth. "Well, I am certain that this won't happen again," said Matt's dad. "Am I right, Matt?"

"Yes, sir," Matt said without paying any attention.

But that was the automatic answer Matt gave whenever his father asked him a question in that tone of voice. Matt hadn't really heard much of anything for the last few minutes. His mind had started spinning as soon as he had heard that Jack Callahan had been expelled.

His first reaction had been, *Ha! Sweet revenge!* But then he realized that Jack would also be seeking revenge. Matt tried to see the bright side. After all, he was going home at one o'clock, and now he had an unexpected day off because of his suspension.

He could tell his parents weren't really that upset with him. He was pretty sure that his father was secretly proud that he had stood up to the school bully.

On the drive home, his father stopped by the scene of the crime to get his backpack out of the dumpster. Thankfully, it was still in there.

Matt sat in the car, waiting for his father. When he looked over at the dumpster, Jack was standing just behind it, staring straight at him, bigger and meaner than ever!

Then, just like that, Jack was gone.

No, I'm seeing things. It's just my imagination, Matt thought.

He turned to look through the back window down the other end of the alley. Jack was standing directly behind the car!

Then again, he just wasn't there. Matt knew he was freaking out.

The car door opened, and Matt's dad got in the front seat.

"Okay, buddy, let's get on home and see if we can try to have a better second half of your birthday," he said as he tossed the backpack into Matt's lap.

The drive home was only a few minutes, but Matt saw Jack hiding in at least three different shadows along the way. He knew he was being ridiculous because he was sure that Jack was still sitting in the principal's office at school.

Matt was paranoid. If it were possible, his life had just become even worse. Jack now had nothing else to do but terrorize him.

ANT FARM

Chapter 4

Matt walked in the front door of his house and was greeted by his sister's dog just like any other day. Except it wasn't a pleasant greeting. Muffy ran at him, showed her teeth, barked viciously, and then retreated to her dog bed.

Man, even animals don't like me, Matt thought.

He hated that dog. Whenever Julia walked into the house, Muffy ran, wagged her tail, stood on her hind legs, and was the nicest dog on the planet. Muffy was nice to everybody except him. Matt had never been mean to the dog. There was just something about Matt that Muffy didn't like. Just like everyone else.

Matt made a little bark at the mutt as he walked down the hall, and the little Yorkshire terrier growled back.

A few hours later, Matt's grandma arrived, carrying a perfectly wrapped gift complete with ribbon, a bow, and a card. Matt rushed to the door with Muffy nipping at his heels.

"How's my little birthday boy?" she said, coming in and giving her standard smothering hug.

"I'm fine," Matt said, hugging her back.

"Oh my goodness, what happened to you?" she said, touching the side of his face.

Matt glanced over briefly at his mother.

"Oh...it's nothing. Me and a buddy of mine were just wrestling, and his elbow hit me by accident."

"That's quite a doozy. Did you take him to see a doctor about it?" she asked Matt's mother.

"Oh, no. The school nurse said it was just a run-of-the-mill black eye. She said as long as his vision was okay, there was nothing to worry about."

After dinner, his mother brought in the cake and presents and set them on the table. "Okay, present time!"

He first opened the presents from his parents. They had given him a neat model tank to build and the newest *Spy Chase* video game.

When he opened Grandma's gift, Matt knew he was going to have to be polite.

Great, another belt-making kit or a new atlas or something, he thought, as he prepared himself to win the Academy Award for best actor.

"Thanks, Grandma," he said as he forced his mouth into a wide grin.

But when he opened the perfectly wrapped present, to his surprise, it actually was something cool. It was an ant farm that you put together yourself. But this one was way cooler than most.

The box had a drawing of a giant ant on the front climbing over buildings with people running and screaming in terror. He turned the box over, and he saw that it really did have a tiny city that the ants could crawl around in.

"This is awesome, Grandma!" Matt shouted with true excitement. "This is gonna be soooo cool. Thanks!"

He gave her a big hug and immediately ran to the middle of the living room floor to open the box.

It was perfect. He now had his own little world to control.

ANT FARM

Chapter 5

Matt spent the rest of the night working on the ant farm. The ants, of course, did not come in the kit, but his grandmother had already ordered them. They would be arriving by overnight mail the next morning. Matt wanted to have everything ready so that his ants could start terrorizing the city as soon as possible.

The first step was to fill the clear plastic container with the five-pound bag of sand that the ants were to live in. The ant farm itself was very different than the tall, thin ones he had seen in the toy store.

This one was about the size of a small TV. It was basically a tall, clear shoebox. After pouring the sand in the bottom, the next step was to construct the city on top of the dirt.

Matt could design the city any way he wanted. There were about twenty-five different buildings that could be attached in any order, including skyscrapers, row homes, stores, and even a football stadium.

Matt spent hours getting everything just right. He wanted it to be perfect for his new friends when they arrived the next day.

Also included in the kit were a large magnifying glass and a huge guide on ant characteristics and behavior. Once the construction was completed, Matt settled into bed with a flashlight and the ant guidebook.

The book was more than a hundred pages, filled with all sorts of information on raising a colony of ants. It had large color pictures of ants from all over the world.

Up close, they were monstrous looking. On their heads, they had giant pinchers called mandibles, which they used to tear their food apart and to fight. They also had stingers on their backsides like bees. These could be used to inject poison into their prey.

The manual warned to handle the ants carefully because they could bite and a sting would be very painful. The book also cautioned against using ants from the backyard because these ants would be too small and could escape. The ants that were being shipped were much larger than ordinary ones.

Matt stared in disbelief, and his jaw hung open as he read the guidebook. He was astonished. It wasn't every day that he got a toy that could inflict pain! He was so excited to get started that he didn't think he would be able to sleep.

It was well past midnight when he finally drifted off with the flashlight still turned on and the book lying on his chest.

That night was a restless one. It seemed that he was awake every hour or so. Finally, Matt decided to go downstairs and get a drink. It was very dark outside, but his parents always left the kitchen light on.

As his foot hit the bottom step, he heard something unusual. It was a clicking sound, as though someone were walking with tap-dancing shoes. And then suddenly, it stopped. Matt froze and tried to keep silent.

Then he heard another noise that sounded like a giant straw slurping the bottom of a soda. Matt took another step forward, and the floorboard creaked loudly. The slurping sound stopped immediately. Matt froze again.

Matt watched in horror as a long, black leg curled slowly around the corner. Two other legs followed, and then Jack's head peered out and stared right at him.

Matt rubbed his eyes, not believing what he was seeing. Slowly, Jack emerged from around the corner and stepped into the hallway. But this wasn't the normal

Jack Callahan. This Jack had retractable mandibles attached to the side of his face and, in addition to his human arms and legs, he had six long jointed legs growing out of his back.

Matt darted out of the front door and into the damp night. It seemed he ran endlessly. Wherever Matt went, Jack would always be there just behind him. Even when he couldn't see him, he could still hear each of his tentacle-like legs clicking on the ground and some sort of slobbering, chewing noise coming from just behind the pinchers.

The creature chased him throughout the neighborhood and eventually back to his house. Matt just barely made it to the front door and managed to slam it behind him just in time.

Matt locked the deadbolt and rested his back against the door. Suddenly, one of the creature's legs scratched him on the side of his neck. It had gotten caught in the door and was stuck.

Matt screamed and ran to the kitchen and returned with a large knife. With one swing, he severed the leg, and it fell to the floor. Jack's cry of pain was not human. It was a terrifying, ear-piercing screech that wouldn't stop.

Just then Matt felt a painful scratch on his leg. Jack's hairy leg was still alive and trying to grab Matt!

Matt frantically kicked it off and swung wildly with the kitchen knife. The leg kept coming, slowly pulling itself across the floor towards him.

He ran and jumped over it, just out of reach of the hairy claw, and ran up the steps to his bedroom. He could hear the pitter-patter of Jack on the roof of the house. The clicking of the feet wasn't quite the same as it was before because now the creature was hurt and only had five legs.

Matt slammed his bedroom door behind him and locked it immediately. He knew the severed leg would be scratching at the door shortly, trying to get in.

Then he saw it.

The leg was coming under the door. He backed away, trying to think of what to do next. The sound on the roof was as loud as ever.

Suddenly, everything became deadly silent. There was no noise coming from the roof, and the severed leg lay completely still. Matt slowly turned to look over his shoulder out his bedroom window.

There, hanging upside down outside the window, was the creature. Blood dripped from the stump that used to be its leg, and saliva oozed from its mouth and onto the mandibles, which were pinching back and forth.

With its human hand, the monster smashed through the window as Matt screamed in horror.

ANT FARM

Chapter 6

Matt woke with a yell and found himself sitting up in bed, soaked from head to toe in sweat. There, at his side, was the flashlight and the ant farm manual.

He looked over to the window; there was nothing but his bobble head collection.

"Man, what a night," he said.

Then he remembered. This was the day his ants would arrive!

What a perfect day to be suspended, he thought.

Matt looked at the clock. It was already nine o'clock. The delivery was supposed to arrive by ten. He quickly got dressed, grabbed the ant farm manual from his bed, and ran downstairs.

"Mom, did my ants arrive yet?" he shouted.

"No, nothing yet, honey."

He sighed and went to the sofa in the sitting room so that he could watch through the front window for the mailman to arrive. He still had about another thirty pages of the manual to read anyway.

About forty-five minutes later, just as he was finishing the last few pages, the delivery truck pulled into the driveway. Matt sprang to his feet and was standing at the end of the walkway before the driver had even opened his door of the truck.

"Wow! You must be expecting something really cool," the driver said.

"Yeah, it's a bunch of ants for my new ant farm I just got for my birthday."

"You mean to tell me I've been driving with a bunch of vicious killers in the back of my van for the past two hours? They could have eaten me alive!" the driver said. "Well, happy birthday."

Matt thanked the man, took the package, and ran up the steps into his house. Because he had already read the manual from start to finish, he knew exactly what to do.

The ants' new home was all set up and waiting for them. The book said that in order to keep them from escaping and possibly biting, the ants should be placed in the refrigerator for about fifteen minutes. This would slow them down and make them less aggressive.

He opened the package. Inside, packed in several layers of plastic bubble wrap, was a long, clear tube a little bit longer than a can of soda.

There they were. These ants were big. Each was about the length of a jelly bean. All of them were as black as coal. He couldn't really see many details of their bodies because they were scurrying around frantically inside the tube.

"Eww, that's disgusting," his mother said, looking over his shoulder. "I can't believe I'm going to have those things inside my house."

"Wait till you see what I get to feed 'em—dead bugs!" he taunted his mom. He held the tube in front of her, dancing around happily.

"I could kill your grandmother. Just please, don't let them get out or you're paying the exterminator bill," his mother said with a slight smile on her face. As much as she didn't like ants in her house, she was very happy to see Matt excited about something. She couldn't remember the last time he was so energized about anything.

Matt ran to the refrigerator, opened the door, and put the ants on the top shelf.

"WHOA! WHAT ARE YOU DOING?" his mom shrieked.

"Aw, Ma, don't worry. I'm supposed to do this to slow them down. That way they won't escape when I transfer them to the ant city. The book said it would only take about fifteen minutes."

"Oh, this is just great," his mom said, shaking her head. "My entire house is being taken over by insects!"

ANT FARM

Chapter 7

Exactly fourteen minutes and fifty-nine seconds later, Matt opened the refrigerator. He had already opened it five other times out of curiosity. Sure enough, just like the book had said, the ants were all barely moving.

Matt carefully picked up the tube so as not to excite them once again and walked quickly up to his room. He immediately opened the lid to the ant city and very delicately poured the ants into the top.

A few of them were trying to resist falling out by clinging to the sides. Matt followed the instructions in the book and gently tapped on the tube with one finger to loosen the ants' grip. It worked like a charm. He had successfully transferred all of them without a single one escaping.

After about ten minutes, the ants were back to normal. They scurried about, trying to make sense of their new surroundings. All but a few, that is, for about five of them had died, either during shipping or while in the fridge.

Several of them immediately began digging tunnels. Matt couldn't take his eyes off of them. He pulled up a chair and used the magnifying glass to see how this was done.

It was incredible. One ant would dig while the others would make one trip after another, each removing a grain of sand and bringing it to the top. This excavated sand became the anthill.

It took a few hours, but eventually the ants had built several tunnels that led to wider cave–like openings. What happened next was amazing.

The ants carried their dead comrades down a tunnel and placed them all in a pile in one of the caves.

Matt wasn't sure if they would eat them later or if this was some sort of burial. Were the ants cannibals? He figured they could be. He decided he should feed them some food rather than wait and find out.

The guide said that the ants would eat almost anything, including bugs, but that fruits and vegetables were their favorites. It also said that sugary foods were a special treat, but the book emphasized—whatever they ate—not to overfeed them. A bit of food the size of a pea was enough to feed all of them for three days!

"Okay, guys, it's dinner time," Matt said. He opened the top of the ant city and placed a small piece of banana right on top of the tallest skyscraper.

Within minutes, an ant had found the food and gone back to tell the others. Matt watched with the magnifying glass as each ant used its mandibles to tear off a small piece and carry it back to the caves.

"Is that good? What should we try next, a dead bug maybe?" Matt said, not expecting an answer. "So how do you guys like the big city?"

"Man, you are crazy!" his sister Julia said as she stood in the doorway, munching on some Pop Rocks, her favorite candy. She had been watching her brother talk to a bunch of ants, sitting with his face six inches away from the ant farm.

"You think you had problems before? Wait till the kids at school see you talking to bugs. They'll really think you're a freak then."

"Yeah, yeah. Leave me alone," Matt said, waving his fingers at her as if to dismiss her from the room. "What are you doing home from school so early anyway? What, let me guess, you got suspended too?"

"Oh, yeah, that's likely," she said. "It's four o'clock. This is the time I always get home."

Matt looked at her in disbelief. He had been in his room, staring at his precious ants and talking to them, for six hours!

"Maybe I am completely nuts," he said. "I've been in my room all day."

Julia walked over to take a closer look.

"Well, I have to hand it to you, they're pretty cool. Not all-day cool, but pretty cool."

"You should have seen them before when I fed them some banana. It was awesome," Matt said.

"What else do they eat?" Julia asked.

"Just about anything, but the book said they love sweets."

"How about some dessert?" Julia said as she lifted up her bag of Pop Rocks.

"Yeah, sure. But just a little bit. They're not supposed to eat too much."

Julia opened the top and tilted the package slightly so that a few of the tiny candies would fall out. Instead, over half of the pouch came spilling out, spreading all over the entire ant metropolitan area. Candy was everywhere!

"I SAID JUST A LITTLE BIT!" Matt yelled.

Matt tried to pick up as many of the pieces as he could, but it was impossible. His fingers were too big to reach the tiny pieces of candy that filled the thin spaces between the skyscrapers. He knew that too much food could kill them, but there was nothing that he could do.

A minute later, the ants were all above ground and fast approaching their deadly banquet.

ANT FARM

Chapter 8

"Look at those things go," Julia said, wide-eyed. "They're ferocious!"

Matt was delighted to have someone else excited about his ants.

"Yeah, they're awesome, especially Anthony there. He seems to be the leader," Matt said.

"You've named your ants?" Julia asked.

"Just that one. He's the biggest, so he's easy to recognize. I can't tell the other ones apart yet. They all look the same."

Just then the first of the ants, Anthony, had reached one of the pieces of pink candy. Matt and Julia watched with the magnifying glass. The ant stopped, then circled around, trying to determine whether or not it was food.

Satisfied with the sugary smell, it steadied the piece in its mandibles and put it up to its mouth.

Through the magnifying glass, Matt and Julia could see the spit oozing from its jaws and onto the candy. The ant began moving his mouth in order to ingest the sweet, syrupy fluid and then...

POP!

The ant was sent hurtling backwards all the way into the next building (which was only about an inch away).

"Whoa! Did you see that?" Matt yelled.

"It looked like he just exploded or something!" Julia said.

Then, like some sort of creature from a horror movie, the ant struggled to his feet and slowly approached the piece of candy once again.

Cautiously, he began the same procedure as before. He picked up the candy and began slobbering on it in order to break it down into a sugary liquid.

ZAP!

Again, the ant was forced backwards through the air, across the entire city street.

"COOL!" Matt and Julia screamed in unison.

"Julia, I think it's the Pop Rocks exploding! The force is like a stick of dynamite to something their size," Matt exclaimed.

"Yeah, you're right. Do you think it can hurt them?"

"Got me," Matt mumbled. This time, the ant didn't waste any time. It scrambled to its feet and ran frantically back to the candy.

"Look, he loves it! He can't get enough," Matt said.

"It's not just him," Julia said. "Look at the rest of them."

Sure enough, every ant, about twenty in total, was doing the same thing. Each was viciously attacking a piece of candy for a few seconds, only to be violently thrown off a moment later. But they loved it.

After several minutes, the intensity of the explosions wore off. Each ant clung to his piece of candy as if it were the last morsel of food on the face of the earth. The ants would flinch every once in a while, but the force wasn't enough to make them lose their grip.

Eventually, the pieces melted away to nothing, and the overstuffed ants waddled back to the anthill, looking like they had just finished Thanksgiving dinner.

After all, the ants had just eaten more food in a day than they were supposed to in an entire week.

Matt had noticed something unexpected. When he fed them the banana, the ants tore it apart and brought it back to the anthill for all to share. According to the book, this was normal ant behavior. But with the Pop Rocks, they ate every last piece right where they found it. The candy caused them to completely lose control of their actions.

By now, every ant had retreated to the tunnels. The few ants that Matt could see underground lay completely motionless.

Julia was really concerned. "Do you think they're sleeping or dying?"

"I don't know, but it doesn't look good, does it?"

The candy was all gone. The ant city was completely wiped clean. Nothing moved.

The ant city was now an ant ghost town.

ANT FARM

Chapter 9

Matt felt terrible for being an ant killer. *Now what do I do?* he thought.

He had spent every possible second watching his tiny pets. All of the ants looked dead. Every once in a while, one of their legs would twitch, which was even worse because it looked like they were suffering.

He knew he could send away for more ants. They really didn't cost that much, but heck, he had only had them for one day.

Matt needed something to keep his mind off the fact that his suspension was just about over. The next morning he had to go back to school.

He didn't know how the other kids would react to him now that he had gotten the school bully expelled. Would they call him a snitch or a hero? He was pretty sure he knew the answer to that.

But more importantly, he still had to get to school and back again with Jack on the loose somewhere out there.

Worrying about Jack—and remembering that he had probably managed to kill all of his ants on the very same day that they had arrived—made for another restless night. Pictures of huge ants and Jack's face kept appearing in his head.

At least three times during the night, he woke with a start. The third time, he grabbed the flashlight from the nightstand and shined it on the ant city across the room. There was still no movement, just as he had figured.

At about two o'clock in the morning, Matt finally fell asleep.

Once again, dreams of Jack terrorized him. By morning, Matt was seconds away from being devoured by Jack as a giant ant. Only the noise of his alarm clock saved him from a gruesome death.

BEEP! BEEP! BEEP! BEEP! BEEP!

"Aw, great," he moaned.

The only thing worse than getting ripped to shreds by a giant ant human was having to go to school.

He reached over and turned off the alarm. It was 7:05. The alarm has been going off for five straight minutes. *Man, I must have been completely knocked out*, he thought.

He got out of bed and shuffled straight to the bathroom, still rubbing the sleep out of his eyes. He splashed water over his face to wake himself and began to brush his teeth.

In the middle of brushing, he stopped suddenly, the toothpaste dripping down his hand.

The ants! he remembered.

He quickly rinsed his mouth and ran out of the bathroom, still drying his face with the hand towel.

When he turned into his room, he could already tell that they were actually still alive! There was movement everywhere. Flashes of black ants scurried over the tall buildings and through the plastic city streets.

As he approached more closely, he started to walk almost in slow motion. He stood there and stared as if he were in a trance. He couldn't believe what he was seeing.

Matt realized why he could tell from all the way across the room that the ants were indeed moving.

"Holy cow," he muttered under his breath.

The ants were definitely still alive and very healthy. They had grown to double their size overnight!

ANT FARM

Chapter 10

     "What in the world?" Matt said under his breath.
     He had never seen ants this big before. They were absolutely enormous, easily the size of large crickets. He was happy that they were even alive. He had been worried that after eating all of those Pop Rocks, they would all be dead.
     Then he remembered the feeding frenzy they were in when they ate the candy.

It must have been the Pop Rocks that made them grow. He was sure of it. How else could this happen in such a short time?

"Hey, buddy," his mom said, standing in the doorway.

Matt spun around and stood in front of the ant city so that she couldn't see. He knew that if his mom saw the Godzilla-sized ants, she would freak out.

"Uhh...hey, Mom."

"Honey, would you like it if I drove you to school for the rest of the week?" His mother knew that Matt would be afraid of another encounter with Jack.

"Yeah, sure. That would be great," he answered. He was relieved that he wouldn't have to face Jack on the walk to school, but he was even happier that his mother hadn't seen the ants.

"Okay, get a move on. We have to leave in fifteen minutes," she said as she headed downstairs.

Matt immediately went over and locked his bedroom door. He looked back at the ant city. He knew he couldn't just leave it out in plain sight on his dresser. There was no way that his mom would let anything this size stay in the house.

He quickly scanned his room for ideas. Finally he focused on the closet. Matt needed a place where the ants would not be discovered. He had a huge closet that was very dark.

He picked up the ant farm and carefully placed it all the way in the back, behind the old clothes that he never wore. He was confident that his mom would never see it back there. He closed the closet doors and quickly got dressed for school.

Just as he was about to head downstairs, a thought occurred to him: *Was that lid on tight?* He wasn't sure if it had been loosened when he had moved the ant city into the closet.

He retrieved the flashlight from his bed and went back to the closet.

Everything was secure.

He couldn't imagine the scene his mom would make if the monstrous ants were able to escape.

ANT FARM

Chapter 11

There was one big topic of conversation at school. Everywhere, kids were talking about Jack being expelled and Matt's black eye.

It was a strange experience for Matt. When he walked down the hall to his locker, groups of students would stop talking for a moment and look at his eye.

But the surprising part was that he wasn't being teased about it. It was almost as if he were being accepted as a normal kid. This was the boy, after all, who fought back against the school bully and lived to tell the tale.

Some kids merely looked, while others actually talked to him.

"What's up, dude?" they said, instead of calling him "wimp" and "loser". One of the bigger kids actually called him "Rocky".

But as exciting as it was to be treated nicely by his classmates, the day seemed to drag on forever. Matt couldn't wait to get home to see his ants. It was the only thing on his mind during all of his classes.

He was thinking about what might happen if he fed them even more Pop Rocks. Would they get even bigger?

The more he thought about it, the more he realized that he must treat it like a secret experiment. He knew that he wasn't supposed to overfeed them and that they could die if he did. Even though they were just ants, it was wrong to deliberately harm them.

But his curiosity was stronger than his guilt. He viewed it as a science experiment. His mind couldn't rest until he saw how much these ants would grow.

At two-thirty, the school bell finally rang. Matt darted out of the front entrance. His mother was waiting there to drive him home. Matt needed more Pop Rocks and had come up with a plan. He opened the car door and hopped in.

"Hey, Mom. Can we make a stop at the Quickmart on the way home? I need some more notebook paper. I'm just about out."

"Okay, I need some milk and bread anyway," she replied.

His mom went and picked up the groceries that she needed while Matt found the notebook paper that he really didn't need. At the checkout counter, he tossed a bag of Pop Rocks next to the milk.

"Can you buy these for me and I'll pay you back when I get home?" he asked.

"I guess one little bag of candy wouldn't do any harm," she answered.

Matt just looked straight ahead to avoid any eye contact. *I sure hope not*, he thought nervously.

ANT FARM

Chapter 12

Matt walked in the front door of his house and, this time, ignored the yipping of his sister's rat-dog. He ran straight upstairs to his room and locked the door behind him.

He opened the closet door and slowly took out the ant city. There they were. They had not grown anymore since the morning, but they were almost as big as some of the buildings in the plastic city. Crawling on top of these structures made them appear that much larger.

"Hey, guys. Did you miss me?" Matt said as if he were talking to a group of friends. "I picked up a special treat for you. I figured you'd like to try cherry-flavored today."

Matt opened the packet of candy. This time, however, he didn't just pour it over the city. He wanted to give them a little bit at a time so that he could more closely observe their behavior.

He picked out a single piece of the candy and held it between his thumb and index finger. With the other hand, he opened up the top of the city. Then he placed the piece right on the fifty-yard line of the football stadium.

It only took a few seconds for the feeding frenzy to begin. But this time, all of the ants were going after the same piece. They formed a giant ball around the candy. When it exploded, the entire ball barely hopped off the ground because the weight of the ants was too great.

After a few minutes, the piece of candy had been completely devoured.

Matt grabbed several more pieces from the bag.

"Did you like that? Want some more? Here ya go."

Then something amazing happened. When Matt reached over the ant city to sprinkle the candy about, the ants raised up on their hind legs.

Matt's hand jumped back for fear that they were trying to bite him. When he moved his hand away, the ants got back down on the ground and followed it to the edge of the container.

Matt realized that they weren't trying to bite him. The ants were just completely focused on the food.

He kept the candy between his two fingers in front of the glass. Then he started to move his hand slowly back and forth.

"Come here. Come on, that's it," he said as if he were training a pet.

Sure enough, the ants followed wherever the candy went. Again, he put his hand over the top of the city, and the ants stood up, begging to be fed.

"Up! Up! Up!" he dangled it just out of their reach.

Then he gave them their reward.

"Good boys! Here you go."

He poured a bunch in and watched them scramble for the pieces. The exploding ant show went on for at least fifteen minutes.

The ants gorged themselves, eating every last bit that could be found. After their feast, one by one they staggered back to the tunnels, where they fell into a sugar stupor. There they lay completely still, except for an occasional leg twitch. Some lay sideways and others flat on their backs; it didn't seem to matter.

Matt's excitement slowly turned to nervousness. He stared at the ant farm, wondering what would happen next. He remembered the information in the ant farm manual that talked about overfeeding the ants. Then he looked at the sticker on the bottom corner of the ant city:

WARNING! Do not handle the ants! They can bite, and they will sting. The sting is painful and will cause swelling. If you are stung, apply ice until the pain subsides. If symptoms persist, consult a doctor.

Geez, what have I done? What if one of them had gotten out?

Just then there was a knock on the door.

"Hey, Matt, open up." Julia was home from school, coming to check on the ants.

Matt quickly put the box back into the closet and covered it up. He knew he'd better not tell her the truth. She would definitely be scared of them and would probably tell his parents.

He opened up the door and tried to look kind of sad.

"Hey, how are the ants?" she said. "Are they all right?"

"No, none of them made it," Matt lied.

"Oh, I'm so sorry. It was my fault," Julia said, upset that she had overfed them.

"It's okay. They're just ants. I can order new ones; it's only a couple of bucks. Plus, it was pretty cool to watch, wasn't it?"

"Yeah," she said, looking down at her feet. "Well, I'll pay for them. Just let me know how much."

Matt thanked her and closed the door behind him. He leaned against the door and stared at the closet, wondering what would happen next.

ANT FARM

Chapter 13

The next day was Saturday, and Matt was grateful to spend the weekend at home. He had not seen Jack Callahan since their fight, but he couldn't relax anywhere else except his very own room.

He awoke fairly early, especially for a Saturday morning. It was about seven o'clock. Immediately, he thought of the ants.

It was still pretty dark in his room because the shades were down. Matt glanced at the closet door, feeling butterflies in his stomach as he thought of what could be behind it.

Would they still be alive?

He was pretty sure they would be. What he wasn't sure of was whether they had grown or not. Maybe the first time was just a coincidence, just a growth spurt.

He lay in the bed, staring at the ceiling, not sure that he wanted to find out.

Everything was very quiet. The sun had already risen slightly, so the crickets were finished chirping for the night. Through his closed window, he could hear a few birds whistling from time to time.

But in the house, not a sound could be heard. He rolled over on his side, still under the covers, and stared at the closet.

Then he heard it. It was a muffled sound that Matt was sure was coming from behind the doors.

He held his breath and lay completely still.

There it was again. It was a scratching sound like Muffy pawing at the door to go outside. But this was definitely coming from the closet.

It's the ants! That's gotta be them moving around. They're alive!

Matt sat up in bed and tossed off the covers. He could still hear the persistent scratching noise. He stood up and flipped on the light switch.

Then a thought occurred to him: *How can I hear ants crawling behind a closed door ten feet away?*

He crept to the door, took a deep breath,
opened it, and walked to the back of the closet.
He couldn't believe his eyes.

ANT FARM

Chapter 14

    The ants were even bigger! Each was almost the size of Matt's finger. What really freaked him out wasn't as much their size, but what they were doing.

    The ants, all twenty of them, were standing up along the side of the ant city. Each was on its hind legs, clawing repeatedly at the plastic box. It was as if they were trying to get out. They looked like dogs scratching on the door, begging to go out for a walk.

    As soon as they saw Matt, they stopped scratching. They continued to awkwardly balance themselves on their back legs as if they wanted to be greeted or fed a snack.

Matt got down on his knees and put his face close to the box to get a better look. The city was not as impressive anymore because the ants were all about the same size as the tallest building. When he kneeled down, the ants got down also.

"Whoa, this is amazing," he said.

The ants all kept staring right at him. If he moved to the left, they all followed. If he rose up, they stood and begged. He was their master.

Matt figured that the Pop Rocks made them grow. He also knew that they saw him as the giver of the wonderful nectar. The Pop Rocks would keep the ants completely under his control.

But there was a problem. It appeared that the ants *needed* the candy. They couldn't live without it. And the bigger they grew, the more they seemed to crave it.

He knew he only had a little bit left from the packet he fed them the day before. As he stood to go back to the dresser to get it, the ants frantically began scratching the plastic again.

"Okay, okay, just a second. I'm getting it," Matt said.

It didn't seem as crazy to be talking to ants anymore now that they were the size of small mice.

Matt held the candy in his hand. There was just a tiny bit left.

"Okay, guys, let's not fight over this," he said. He dumped the remainder of the pack into the top of the city. It didn't last very long.

There weren't enough pieces for each ant to have his own, so two or three ate one tiny piece at a time. Within minutes, everything had been entirely devoured. But when it was gone, they were not at all satisfied.

The ants turned toward Matt once again, begging for more. Each one stood tall on its sticklike legs. Now that they were bigger, it looked like they had little knees and feet. Their bodies looked like his fingernails painted black, hard and shiny. He could see the stingers dangling from their abdomens like spears. Their powerful jaws snapped shut as they tried to bite through the plastic wall.

"Sorry, guys, that's all I've got."

It didn't matter. The ants needed more. They had to have it, and they would do anything to get it. They scratched and clawed at the plastic, desperately hoping their master would feed them again.

Matt knew he had a problem on his hands. He had to give them more, a lot more.

He pushed the ant farm to the back of the closet again. The ants became even more crazed when they realized that the food was not forthcoming.

He closed the door and said, "I'll be right back. I'll go as fast as I can."

As he started to head downstairs, Matt could still hear the ants scratching. The sound could be heard clear out into the hallway.

He went back to his room to try to find a way to muffle the noise. He knew if anyone discovered two-inch-long ants in his room, that person would be scared to death! He reached into his hamper and took out an armload of dirty clothes. Then he tossed them on top of the ant city.

He closed the closet door and then closed his bedroom door. The sound was still slightly audible.

I'll just have to go quickly, he thought.

He bounded down the stairs with his money in his pocket.

"Ma! I'm going outside for a little while! See ya later!" he shouted.

He jumped on his bike and took off down the street. He was so concerned about the ants that he didn't give a second thought to Jack Callahan.

ANT FARM

Chapter 15

     In less than five minutes, Matt was at the store. He had no time to lose. He hopped off of his bike, leaving it right in the middle of the sidewalk, and ran into the store.

     "Hey, what's the hurry, Matthew? It's the weekend," said Mr. Stoops, the owner.

     "Oh, good morning, Mr. Stoops," Matt replied. "I'm just glad not to be in school, that's all."

     Matt walked down the candy aisle. There were only two packs left! Would that be enough? He quickly brought them to the counter and gave Mr. Stoops the money. Then he stashed them in his backpack and went back outside to his bike. Five minutes later, he was back home.

Mission accomplished, he thought. *I hope Mom didn't hear the scratching noise and go check it out. That would be an ugly scene.*

He left his bike in the driveway and ran in through the front door.

Immediately he knew something was wrong. He could hear Muffy, the rat-dog, yipping nonstop.

"MUFFY...MUFFY... STOP THAT BARKING!" his mother yelled from downstairs.

But she didn't stop. Matt stood just inside the doorway trying to figure out exactly what the problem was. The dog just wouldn't quit. Something really had her upset.

Then Matt realized that the barking was coming from inside his room.

THE ANTS! That's what she's barking at!

Matt was scared. He didn't know if Muffy was just aggravated by the scratching noises or if she had gotten into the closet.

He darted up the stairs and, sure enough, the door to his room was ajar.

I know I closed it to cover up the noise, he thought. *Muffy must have pushed it open.*

There was the rat-dog, frantically barking and scratching at the closet doors.

"Hey! Hey, stop it! Come here!" Matt commanded.

Muffy turned and looked at Matt, then went right back to barking and scratching again.

Matt took off his backpack and tossed it on the bed. He walked quickly over to the closet and picked up the dog.

"Hey, stop barking, you little rat."

As he picked her up, Muffy turned, snarling and growling, and bit him right on the hand. It was hard and vicious enough to break the skin.

"OWWW!" Matt screamed in pain, dropping the dog on the floor and grabbing his hand. "I HATE YOU!" he yelled angrily.

The dog tore out of the room and down the stairs, knowing that she had done something wrong. Matt removed his hand that was covering the wound to examine it. It wasn't horrible, but there were three of four punctures between his thumb and his wrist. There was enough blood that he knew he should get his mother to look at it.

Then he thought, *How do I explain what the dog was barking at in my closet?* His mom would definitely check it out to see what was irritating Muffy in the first place.

Matt decided that he'd better feed the ants soon to calm them down. His mother may have heard him yell and would come to investigate. He needed them to be quiet.

Quickly and in pain, Matt got one of the packets of candy out of his backpack and crawled back into the closet. With his good hand, he removed the pile of dirty clothes covering the top of the ant city.

It was difficult to open the packet because he had to use both hands. It was painful, but he managed to do it. He opened the lid of the box and poured the candy right on top of the circle of ants, which were standing awkwardly and begging to be fed. Along with the Pop Rocks, some blood dripped onto several of the buildings and onto the ants themselves.

Matt closed the lid and tossed some of the dirty clothes back on top of the ant city. He shut the closet door and then stood in front of it, listening.

Finally, they've calmed down, he thought.

He looked down at his hand. The blood was still coming, but the pain wasn't that bad as long as he kept pressure on the wound.

He went to the bathroom and began to clean it up. With three Band-Aids, he was able to cover the bite and eventually stop the bleeding. He made the decision that it was probably better that his mother didn't find out. The fewer questions she asked, the better.

Now that everything was calm, Matt went back to the closet to observe his pets. They were just finishing up the feast and were moving very slowly.

Several of the buildings were dotted with drops of blood from Matt's wound. The bright red streaks stood in stark contrast to the white structures. The drops had run down into the street, creating an effect like a horror movie. It appeared that a gruesome murder had been committed by these monstrous beasts roaming the city.

All of the candy had been eaten. Not a single piece could be found. Then something truly disgusting happened.

The ants turned their attention to the buildings streaked with blood. They were drinking it as though it were water. They wiped the city clean. It was dessert time, and they were having blood...human blood...Matt's blood.

ANT FARM

Chapter 16

Matt was snoring loudly the next morning. He had been up very late the evening before since it was a Saturday night. He probably would have slept much longer if he had not been awakened unexpectedly.

It was eight in the morning when he felt something gently stroke his neck. He brushed it away the first three or four times out of pure instinct. It took a minute or two for him to realize that it was morning.

He rolled over on his side and slowly opened his eyes. There, on his bed, a few inches from his face, was one of the ants. It was almost as big as his hand!

Matt screamed and pushed it away so that it landed on the floor. He scrambled to the corner of the bed and clutched the covers all around him as protection.

"AAHHH! WHAT THE HECK?" he yelled.

The ant he had knocked on the floor was right back on top of the bed, along with three others. Their eyes protruded like shiny black pearls. The weight of them was enough that he could feel the hard legs through the covers as they walked across him. Their mandibles jutted out at him, moving back and forth as they crawled up onto his chest. Matt was scared to death. They were loose!

Matt looked down on the floor. The rest of them were coming quickly across the carpet, right to the bed. He was terrified, and he was starting to breathe fast.

It was all he could do not to scream so that no one would hear him. He kicked his feet wildly under the covers, trying to keep them away.

But they had already stopped coming any closer. When they reached his feet, they began to stand on their hind legs again.

Wait a minute, they're coming to get fed again, he thought. *The ant was just waking me up.*

Matt tried to calm down. He didn't want to get them upset, but he knew he had to give them food quickly.

"Okay, guys, you want breakfast?" he asked nervously.

He stood up on his bed and walked around the edge, carefully trying to avoid stepping on them. The ants followed obediently. He hopped off his bed and went to the dresser drawer where he kept the candy.

There it was, the last packet. The ants scurried down the side of the bed and over to Matt's feet. At the same time, they all began begging. Matt wanted to get them back to the closet and into the ant city. Then a thought occurred to him: *There's no way they'll be able to move in there.*

They needed a bigger home. He decided to feed them first and to figure out where to put them afterwards. He took the candy and led the ants back to the closet. That's when he saw what had happened.

The entire lid of the ant city was on the floor!

There was only one way it could have happened. They had grown so big that they were able to force it off themselves!

I definitely need to find a bigger box, he thought. He sprinkled some of the Pop Rocks on the floor of the closet to buy him some more time. Then he looked around the room.

His toy chest would be a perfect new home for his pets. As the ants ate, he removed every single toy in the box and threw it on the carpet. When it was empty, he poured the rest of the candy into the bottom of the box.

The ants hungrily climbed into their new home. Once they were all in, Matt closed the lid and pushed it to the back of the closet where the ant city had been kept.

After it was in place, he stacked a pile of books on top to keep them from escaping again. He was sure that they wouldn't be able to get out now. Just to be certain, however, he shut the closet door behind him.

There's no way they can get out of a closed door...I think.

ANT FARM

Chapter 17

Matt had two problems. First, he had to get a ton of sand into the toy chest for the ants to live in. Secondly, he had to get more Pop Rocks. If he had bought the very last pack in the store on Saturday, Mr. Stoops would probably still be out on Sunday.

His mom and dad were at the breakfast table drinking coffee and reading the Sunday paper.

"Morning, sport," his dad said.

Just then Julia came into the room.

"Muffy? Come on, girl. Where are you?" she called. "Mom, where could she be?"

"I don't know, honey. Have you checked down in the basement?"

"Yeah," Julia said, looking worried. "I can't find her anywhere."

"I'll go outside and look around," Matt said. He didn't really care where the dog was. He just wanted to go outside to search for some sand or dirt he could use for the ants.

When he went around to the backyard, he found the perfect spot. The old sandbox hadn't been used in years. There was more than enough sand in it to fill the toy chest. The challenge was going to be getting it inside and unnoticed. He found a bucket and a shovel under the deck and began filling it up.

He managed to sneak back through the front door without being seen. Over the course of the next two hours, he made ten trips to the sandbox. Finally he managed to complete the ants' new home.

It was a scary feeling handling the ants. He didn't want to just cover them with sand for fear that they would be buried alive. So he had to pick up each one and place him on top of the pile after every bucket was poured.

Each one was about the size of his hand. That was scary enough, but what was worse was that they kept twitching. The mandibles were so big, they looked like they could bite one of his fingers off. The hairy legs moving in his palm felt totally disgusting.

Now that he had moved them, he had to figure out a way for his parents to take him to another store.

He was completely out of candy and knew he would need more for the next morning.

He went downstairs and found his mom; she was the easiest target.

"Hey, Mom, are you going shopping anywhere today?"

"No, honey, we've got a lot of work to do around the house."

"How about the grocery store?"

"Just went yesterday. Why? What do you need?"

"Oh...just some more pencils for school. I'm all out."

"Not to worry, I have a whole new pack you can have."

"Uh...great!" he said, trying not to show his disappointment.

Just then Julia came around the corner. "MU¬FFFFY!" she called, hoping to get a response. "COME HERE, MUFFY. WANT TO GO FOR A WALK?"

There was no answer.

"Mom, I've looked everywhere. She must have gotten out when someone opened the door. I'm going outside to look around for her," Julia said, teary-eyed.

Even though he couldn't stand the little rat-dog, Matt was getting a little worried too. He could see that Julia was getting upset.

But Matt had a bigger problem to deal with. He had to get his hands on some more Pop Rocks soon. He could only hope that the corner store would get more in the next day.

If not, how could he possibly control the ants?

ANT FARM

Chapter 18

"Honey, will you go outside with Julia and help her look for Muffy?" his mom asked.

Matt was torn. He really wanted to help Julia, but walking around the neighborhood with Jack trying to kill him wasn't a good feeling.

His father, sensing his fear, said, "You know, I think I'll join you guys. We'll find her in no time with the three of us looking."

In a few minutes, Matt, Julia, and their dad were walking down the sidewalk, each holding a bone or a toy and calling, "MUUFFFY...COME HERE, GIRL!"

When they turned the corner, Matt realized where he was. Jack's house was at the end of the street.

Normally, he wouldn't venture anywhere near this place, but today, he was with his father. He was nervous, but not scared.

As they approached, Matt stopped calling for the dog. Jack's house was a wreck. Besides needing a fresh coat of paint for the past ten years, the yard—if you could call it a yard—was dotted with pieces of junk.

It was difficult to call it a yard because there were only about five small patches of grass in sight. The rest was just dirt and trash.

The reason for the yard being torn up was tied to a tree with a rope. A huge Rottweiler at the other end of the rope was barking viciously as they approached the house. The rope was old and tattered, and with the beast straining to get at them, they decided they'd better cross to the other side of the street.

"That dog looks like it wants to tear us apart," said Julia.

"Hey, isn't that your good friend Jack's house?" asked my dad sarcastically.

"Yep, even his dog is a jerk," I said. "Let's get out of here."

"Yeah, I think Muffy would have enough sense not to venture down by these parts," said Matt's dad. "He'd make a nice appetizer for Killer over there."

Then a thought occurred to Matt: *What if Jack had done something to Muffy?* He was evil enough that if he had found her outside, he might hurt her just to get back at him.

All of a sudden, Matt had the horrible feeling that Jack must have taken Muffy out of their yard. After all, there was no way that she could jump the fence, and they had already checked to see if there were any holes she could have escaped through.

They returned home without any hope of finding her. His father's joke about Muffy being a tasty appetizer for Jack's monster dog wasn't that funny anymore.

ANT FARM

Chapter 19

  The next morning, Matt woke up to the alarm clock to start a new week of school. He didn't hear any noise coming from the closet. What he didn't know was if they were asleep or whether their new home made for a quieter hiding place.

  The one thing he was sure of was that he didn't want to open the lid to check. He didn't have any candy left, so he didn't want to get them excited.

  The ants would have to wait until he got home from school. He prayed that the corner store would have more Pop Rocks. Matt quietly got dressed and opened his bank. He took out the last of his money that he had gotten for his birthday. He was going to spend it all on more candy. He figured that would last for at least a week.

  Wow, this could get expensive, he thought.

"Good morning, sunshine," his mom said as Matt came down the stairs. She was just putting pancakes on the table. "Perfect timing."

"Thanks, Ma, do you have any syrup?" he asked.

Julia was already sitting and waiting for her breakfast. Her elbows were on the table, and her chin rested in her hands.

"Still no Muffy, huh?" Matt asked.

"No, it's hopeless," she said, looking like she was going to cry.

"I'll help you look after school. Maybe we could put up some signs," Matt said, certain that a search would be hopeless.

"Yeah, thanks. It's worth a shot."

"Okay, kids, eat up," his mother said. "Julia, do you want to ride with us to school, or would you rather walk?"

Matt quickly responded, "Oh, no, you don't have to drive me anymore. Everything's cool now. I'll walk to school."

Matt definitely did not want to be driven today. It was extremely important that he get to the corner store on the way home. He couldn't count on his mother taking him.

He had to risk running into Jack Callahan.

"Are you sure? I really think I should drive you. It's really no problem."

"Yeah, I'm sure. Don't worry, I'll be fine."

Just to be safe, he rode his bike. He wanted a little extra speed in case a quick escape became necessary.

School seemed to last forever. Matt couldn't stop worrying that his mother might hear the ants and go into his closet.

Finally the dismissal bell rang, and Matt tore out of the building. He grabbed his bike and rode straight across the street and continued right through the grocery store parking lot. He proceeded up the alley, not giving even a second thought as to whether Jack Callahan would be there again.

Sweating and breathing hard, he dropped his bike and walked into the corner store.

There it was, the black rectangular box with the fluorescent neon green writing on it. It was a brand-new carton of Pop Rocks!

Matt picked out five packets and carried them to the counter. He pulled out all of his money and handed it to Mr. Stoops.

A minute later, he was bounding out of the store, right into a big problem. His bike was pretty much in the same spot that he had left it. Only it wasn't lying on the sidewalk anymore. It was standing straight up, and Jack Callahan was sitting on it.

"Hey, loser," the bully greeted him.

There were enough people around that Matt really wasn't scared.

"Hey, get off my bike, jerk," Matt said angrily. "Give it back."

"This isn't your bike. I found it right in the middle of the sidewalk. Someone threw it away like a piece of trash."

"Give it back, Jack."

"Aw, you can have yer stinkin' bike," Jack said as he got off and walked it over to Matt. "I don't want it nohow. But I will take these!" He snatched the packets of candy out of Matt's hand and at the same time jumped back on the bike and took off.

Matt ran after him for a few steps but soon thought better of it. Then he looked down. Jack had dropped one of the packs.

Thank goodness, he thought.

He had spent all of his money. This pack would have to last a while. He ran home as fast as he could and went straight up to his room.

Matt sat on the edge of his bed with his head in his hands. He didn't know how to tell his parents about his bike. It made him feel ashamed and foolish that he couldn't protect himself. Finally, he burst into tears.

The ants must have heard him because immediately they began scratching the inside of the toy chest. He took his one packet of Pop Rocks and went over to the closet. After wiping away his tears, he opened the closet door and opened the lid.

Matt gulped. They were huge! Each ant was at least six inches long. They stood up, begging for their treat, which Matt hurriedly gave them. Immediately they began to eat.

Amazed, he stood there with the lid open and watched them devour their snack. Now that they were the size of guinea pigs, they looked like creatures from outer space.

Eventually he closed the lid and piled the stack of books back on top to keep them from escaping. Then he sat down on the floor with his back against the toy box and let out a loud sigh.

His thoughts returned to Jack and his bike.

"I hate him. I wish he were dead!" he said out loud.

ANT FARM

Chapter 20

The ants were angry. And they were hungry. That was not a good combination.

They had grown both in size and in brain capacity. All ants already had an amazing ability to communicate with each other. These ants, however, were developing an understanding of the world around them.

They knew that their master was upset. They felt his fear and hatred. They had become aware of all of his emotions.

And they were his personal servants, his own private army.

Matt had been lying in bed, listening to the scratching, for the past ten minutes. He wanted to save the candy to feed them in the morning so that it would sedate them while he was at school.

It was nerve-racking for him to listen to them beg for food and not give it to them. He knew he was doing the right thing by making them wait, but he felt guilty denying them.

Then, all at once, the scratching stopped.

Phew, maybe they've finally fallen asleep, he thought.

He rolled over as quietly as possible so they wouldn't hear him. Five minutes later, he had fallen asleep also.

But the ants hadn't gone to sleep. They had not been begging for food. The scratching noise wasn't the claws on the side of the chest. It was their mandibles tearing away at the side of the wooden container.

They had eaten a hole through the toy box! They had continued digging straight through the dry wall of his closet and into the outside of the house.

The noise had stopped not because they were tired. It had stopped because they had made it to the outside.

The line of ants ran from the second floor down to the backyard. They were free!

But freedom was not what they were after. They were seeking food...and revenge.

* * *

The Rottweiler was the first to see them coming. At first, the dog barked and pulled on the rope to get to its midnight snack. But the ants had but one purpose in mind. They continued straight through, into the dog's circle and towards the house.

The dog lunged at the lead ant, grasping it in his jaws. The ant sunk its powerful mandibles into the side of the dog's mouth, and the animal howled in pain. The Rottweiler retreated with a high-pitched whimper as the ants charged on.

Jack was lying in his bed with his headphones on, listening to an iPod that he had stolen from a kid at school, when the ants reached his house. Without hesitation, they climbed swiftly and quietly up the side of the home, right outside of Jack's bedroom wall.

The ants had little trouble chewing through the wood siding. Large splinters and sawdust fell to the ground as if a chainsaw were cutting through an old log.

Jack thought he heard something. He turned off his music but left the headphones on. The noise appeared to be coming from the backyard. *Must be the dog digging at the side of the house again*, he thought.

"Hey, Rocco! Cut it out!" he yelled. But the scratching continued. *Whatever*, thought Jack. *Let him dig up the stinkin' yard. What do I care?* He switched his music back on.

The ants had now eaten through to the pink insulation between the walls and devoured it like cotton candy. In a matter of seconds, they were working on the inside wall, knowing that their prey lay just a few feet away.

There it was again, thought Jack. It sounded like it was right outside his window. This time, he sat up in bed and took the earphones off. Then he saw it. The wall was moving.

"What the...?"

The wall seemed to explode. The giant pinchers of the lead ant burst through, and the rest of its body poured out after it. The other ants followed. From across the room, it looked as though some sort of black oil were gushing down the wall and onto the floor. But he realized quickly that this wasn't a leak.

Jack jumped on top of his bed and tried to kick the ants away as they climbed up the covers. The first one was knocked back onto the floor, but the second sunk its mandibles into Jack's ankle and held on as Jack screamed and kicked wildly.

A few seconds later, his legs were covered with the hard, black monsters. By the time the last ants were to the bed, his entire body was covered with them.

For the first two minutes, he fought to get away. But they were just too big and their mandibles too powerful. Ten minutes later, there was nothing left except for the iPod and the headphones.

The room had been torn apart from the struggle. The sheets and blankets were ripped from the bed, and blood stained the carpet and mattress. But Jack was gone.

The ants retreated silently back to their home. They climbed up the side of the house back to the comfort of the toy chest for a well-needed rest.

They would not need any Pop Rocks tonight.

ANT FARM

Chapter 21

By the next morning, Matt still hadn't told his parents about his bike being stolen. He didn't want to talk about it because it made him upset. He was embarrassed.

He wanted to walk to school again. He had found enough loose change in the sofa cushions to buy another pack of Pop Rocks on the way home. He figured he could stash the pack in his underwear. There was no way Jack would be able to find it there!

As he stepped out of the front door, a police car went by with its lights blinking and siren wailing. Another followed a few seconds later. They were traveling in the direction Matt used to walk to school, before Jack started picking on him.

He decided to go the old way through the woods so that he could see what was happening.

There's no way Jack would be up this early since he didn't have to go to school, thought Matt. *Plus, there are a couple of police cars down the street. What could be safer?*

As he neared the entrance for the shortcut through the woods, Matt spotted the two police cars. They were a few houses down the street.

Jack's house.

He had to see what was going on. He approached cautiously, trying not to be noticed, just in case Jack had been watching the scene from outside. Both police cars still had their lights flashing. They were parked diagonally facing each other, blocking the street.

Just beyond them, lying in the gutter, was Matt's bike. Matt decided to go and retrieve it while he had the chance.

As he got closer, he could see one of the police officers on the front lawn looking up at the second floor of the house. The other officer was inside, looking through the window down at his partner.

Matt saw what they were looking at. Right in the front of the house, about twelve feet high, was a jagged hole about the size of a Frisbee. It looked like a cannonball had been shot right through the wall. The wood around it was torn to shreds.

Matt picked up his bike and pedaled away unnoticed.

Whatever had happened at that house, he thought, *it couldn't have happened to a better person.*

ANT FARM

Chapter 22

Matt made it to school without a problem. Jack wasn't going to bother him today. He parked his bike and made it to homeroom just before the bell rang. After the announcements and the Pledge of Allegiance, it was off to English.

Matt's English teacher, Mrs. Hartman, was nice enough. In fact, she was the only teacher who ever seemed to notice that he was there. Maybe that was because she had lived a few houses down from Matt his entire life.

She was tall, blonde, and had a very heavy Southern accent, like a country western singer. As long as you did your work and didn't act up in class, her assignments weren't that bad. But like most English teachers, she could be tough.

Mrs. Hartman stood in the doorway as the students approached the classroom.

"Put your research papers on the desk, children, and then you may begin today's grammar drill on the board," she said.

Matt was still out in the hallway when he heard this, and he stopped dead in his tracks. The color immediately flushed from his face. He didn't have his paper. It had been assigned three weeks ago, and he hadn't done a thing! He felt like he were having a bad dream.

He had been just plain lazy for the first week and a half. But then he got suspended, and once the ants arrived, he had thought of nothing else. Now he had no idea what he was going to do.

His mind was spinning. Several different lies went through his head, but none of them seemed believable. He had a five-page research paper due and had nothing to show for it.

Matt walked into the class and went directly to his seat. Everyone else had put his paper on the stack on the corner of the desk.

Then an idea came to him. He could lie and say that he turned it in and it must have been stolen. He knew that this was wrong, but he didn't know what else to do.

For the remainder of the class, Matt fidgeted nervously. All he could think about was the lie he was going to tell. His misery came to an end when the dismissal bell rang.

On the way out, Mrs. Hartman called him back.

"Matt, could I speak with you for a moment?"

Matt's heart began to race, and he could feel a knot forming in his stomach.

"Uh...sure," he said as he walked over, trying to avoid eye contact.

"I didn't get your paper on my desk. Did you forget to turn it in?"

"Uh, no, ma'am. I turned it in. I put it right on your desk. It's right near the bottom of the stack."

"Well, let's just check."

She flipped through the pile of thirty or so reports. The sweat was beginning to form on Matt's forehead.

"Nope, I don't see it," she finally said. "Are you certain that's the answer you want to give me?"

"Somebody must have taken it! I put it there right when I walked into class!"

"Matthew, I saw you come into class. I also watched you walk right past my desk without putting your paper on it and go directly to your seat. Now, are you sure you didn't leave it home or in your book bag?"

Matt knew that she was trying to give him a second chance. He also could tell that she knew he was lying.

He looked down at his feet.

"Well...I'll check. But I'm pretty sure I turned it in," he said with his voice quivering.

"Why don't you go home and look for it? Think very hard about it and see me in the morning."

Matt turned and headed for the door. He felt like crying.

There's no way I can finish an entire research paper in one night, Matt thought. *Man, I'm really gonna get in trouble this time.*

ANT FARM

Chapter 23

Matt made two stops on the way home. First he went by the corner store and bought a packet of Pop Rocks. The ants would surely be hungry when he got home.

Then he walked another couple of blocks to the library. Although he didn't even have a topic picked to write about, he thought he should at least attempt to complete the assignment.

As he walked in the front door of the library, it occurred to him.

ANTS! That's the perfect topic, he thought. *I already know just about everything about them!*

He went and found every book on ants he could find and checked them out. Then he went to the pay phone in the lobby and called his mother.

"Hey, Ma, I've got a paper I need to work on, so I'll be at the library for a while, okay?"

"All right, honey. What time do you think you'll be home?"

"About six."

"Just be home before dark."

"All right. Bye, Mom."

Matt found a table in the corner and began working. He went through the books and started his outline. After what he thought was a short period of time, he noticed it was almost dark outside. He looked up at the clock on the wall. It was already six-thirty, and he still hadn't written a single word yet.

He quickly packed up his books and hopped on his bike for home. By the time he made it there, he realized that it was hopeless. There was no way to write and type a five-page paper in one night.

He trudged up the stairs, carrying the huge pile of books and dumping them in the middle of the bedroom floor. He plopped down on the bed and stared at the ceiling.

"What an idiot! What am I gonna do now?" he said.

The ants had begun scratching away as soon as they heard Matt enter the room. Matt knew he had to feed them, but his mind was in turmoil at the thought of failing English. Worse than that, he had lied to his teacher about it. He was going to be in huge trouble.

Stupid Mrs. Hartman, Matt thought. *She's so mean. Like I have nothing better to do than write a five-page paper. I bet she didn't have that much homework to do when she was a kid.*

He lay in bed feeling sorry for himself and fighting back the tears. Logically, he knew that it was his fault that he had forgotten about the assignment. But he was mad at himself, so he became mad at Mrs. Hartman.

"God, I hate her!" he said under his breath. Finally, he started to cry.

Then he heard it. Actually, he stopped hearing it. The scratching had ceased. He had gotten used to the constant din, and now there was silence. He figured that they had finally gotten tired and fallen asleep.

That's strange, he thought. *It's not like them to go to sleep without eating.*

He got up and got the Pop Rocks out of the backpack. Quietly, he approached the closet and opened the door. He wanted to check on them, but he didn't want to disturb them if they were sleeping.

Carefully he lifted the lid of the toy box a tiny crack. There were no signs of movement. He opened it farther until he could see the entire inside of the chest.

But there was nothing to see. Inside the box was just a pile of sand. He considered the possibility that they had dug down underneath, but they were so big that he didn't think they would fit.

He raked the sand with his fingers so that he wouldn't disturb them if they were sleeping. As Matt brushed across the grains of sand, he felt something hard. When he dug his fingers a bit deeper, he noticed a flash of blue.

He reached down to pick it up and instinctively jumped backwards out of fear and disgust.

He had discovered something truly horrible.

ANT FARM

Chapter 24

Buried in the sand was Muffy's dog collar—with Muffy still wearing it. The blue collar stood in stark contrast to the creamy white color of the dog's skull.

There was only one way Muffy could have gotten in the sand; she had been buried by the ants.

"Whoa, man! What the...?" *They ate her! The ants attacked her and ate her!*

Matt was truly disgusted. He tugged on the collar. After a few yanks, the skeleton came free from its burial ground. The entire carcass was completely intact. The sand quickly filled in the hole left by Muffy.

As the sand poured from the sides into the void, another object became visible. Matt knelt down, holding the dog skeleton by the collar, and stared at the lump that had developed in the sand.

He didn't want to find out what it was. But he knew he had to.

Matt gently set the dog skeleton down on the floor. Then he pulled out a sock from his dresser and put his hand in it like a glove.

As he brushed the yellow sand away from the object, he saw the area around it was red. The more he brushed away, the darker red the sand became.

Finally, he saw what else was in the sand. It was a finger. It wasn't a bone of a finger; this was newer. Matt brushed away more bloody sand. Another finger. Then he realized that it was an entire hand!

Matt uncovered more. On the wrist was a tie-dyed rubber band. Matt recognized it immediately as the one Jack had stolen from him. It was Jack's hand.

He felt his stomach clench and had to fight the urge to throw up.

"They ate Jack too!" he whispered.

Then he saw it.

The hole in the side of the box. He leaned over and tilted his head sideways to get a better look. He could see all the way to the outside of the house. He remembered seeing the same kind of hole once before, on the side of Jack's house.

Matt realized that the ants, over the past few days, had had the freedom to go wherever they pleased. Disgusted, Matt slammed the lid closed. He didn't want to find anything else.

And then a thought occurred to him: *They were protecting me. Muffy had bitten my hand and the next day was missing. Jack stole my bike, and the police were at the house the next morning.*

Matt remembered how upset he had been both of those times. How he had cried because of Jack and yelled at the dog when he was bitten.

They know what I'm thinking, he thought. *I got upset, and they must have felt it! It was simple revenge!*

Matt was afraid. The ants were gone, and they were obviously dangerous. He wasn't sure if they would kill by their own free will or if they only did it to protect him.

Suddenly, a terrible thought crossed his mind. The ants had been in the closet just a few minutes ago. And then, just like that, everything was quiet. He had been angry and crying because of his English assignment.

He was mad at Mrs. Hartman.

The ants were out in the neighborhood, and now they too were mad at Mrs. Hartman.

ANT FARM

Chapter 25

Matt was in his room, staring at his closet.

What the heck do I do now? he thought. His mind was racing. Twenty ants nearly a foot long were on the hunt for his English teacher, and it was his fault.

It was nine o'clock, and it was just about his bedtime. Matt went downstairs and, as normally as possible, told his parents that he was going to bed.

"Okay, dear, see you in the morning," said his mom.

"Don't let the bedbugs bite," said his dad.

Matt walked slowly out of the room and, when he was out of sight, bounded up the stairs. Once in his bedroom, he arranged the pillows under the covers so it appeared that he was in bed. Then he stuffed the packet of Pop Rocks in his pocket, turned off the light, and closed his bedroom door behind him.

Quietly, he crept down the stairs and opened the front door. Minutes later, he was running in the direction of Mrs. Hartman's house.

He figured if he knew where she lived, then the ants knew also. And her house was only just down the road. What he didn't know was how long it would take them to get there. He was pretty sure they would have already arrived.

A couple of minutes later, Matt arrived at the house. Everything was quiet. Only a single light in the living room was on.

Matt crouched by the window and listened for any movement. He didn't hear the familiar clicking sounds of his ants. And he didn't see Mrs. Hartman anywhere.

He walked around to the front of the house to investigate, but there were no signs of life. Then he noticed that there was no car in the driveway.

She isn't home! Thank goodness, he thought. *But where could she be?*

Then Matt remembered the research papers. The huge pile that sat on her desk.

She's probably still at school, he thought.

He darted across the street towards the trail through the woods. Matt hadn't taken the shortcut to school for six months for fear of Jack. And that was during the daylight.

Tonight, he couldn't see more than ten feet in front of him in the dark woods. But he had to get there before the ants did.

ANT FARM

Chapter 26

Mrs. Hartman had stayed late and was in her classroom grading the research papers. She didn't usually stay at school past dark, but she had thirty papers to read and the classroom was where she worked best.

She sat at her desk with the stack of papers in front of her. The comments and corrections on the papers were made with red ink. Some were so poorly written and there was so much red on them that they looked like they were splattered with blood.

Every once in a while, she heard the janitor down the hall cleaning the floors. She couldn't, however, hear the silent stampede of feet coming across the playground.

It went unnoticed when they scampered up the brick wall outside her classroom. But then she heard the chewing and scraping sounds just on the other side of the window frame.

Her writing paused for a moment. She looked over to the window and tried to determine what it could be. The noise was still there, but nothing could be seen through the window.

She stood and slowly walked over, expecting to see some sort of animal run away across the blacktop.

Then she saw the wood of the window frame start to move. At first, a small amount of sawdust started falling. A few seconds later, woodchips were dropping onto the classroom floor.

She took a few steps closer. Suddenly, the hole opened up, and the first ant stuck its head through. Mrs. Hartman let out a gasp and took a few steps backwards, her eyes wide with fear.

The ant kept gnawing at the wood around its head until finally it came charging out of the hole. The rest of the ants followed directly behind. They were coming at her full speed.

* * *

Matt made it out of the woods and stopped once the school was in sight. From a distance, he could see a light on in one of the classrooms, but he couldn't tell if it was his English class.

He sprinted across the playground towards the blacktop.

As he ran, he thought, *What do I tell her when I get there? She'll never believe that a bunch of killer ants are out to eat her because I didn't do my paper.*

He knew it didn't matter whether she believed him. He figured as long as he were with Mrs. Hartman, the ants would obey him.

Once on the blacktop, he could see the hole in the wall. They were already inside.

Matt made it to the window only to see a three-foot-high mound of ants. His pets. They formed a giant ball in the middle of the classroom. All that could be seen was a sea of black limbs and mandibles fighting for a better position.

Matt ripped open the packet of candy and reached his arm through the hole. He poured the Pop Rocks onto the tile floor, and they bounced like sleet on the road.

But the ants didn't notice. Either that, or they didn't care. They were intent on finishing their meal, and nothing could stand in their way.

ANT FARM

Chapter 27

Matt took off running across the playground. Ten minutes later, he was back at home, sweaty and scared.

He knew that he was responsible for the deaths. He didn't hurt anyone, but the ants had killed to protect him.

Besides the terrible scene that he had just witnessed, he was afraid of whom they would go after next.

Who else have I had bad thoughts about? he wondered.

Matt knew that the ants had to be destroyed. They were simply too dangerous and uncontrollable.

More people would get hurt, and who knew how big they would become?

And then an even scarier idea came to his mind. *If the ants can understand my emotions, maybe they also know my thoughts. And if they know my thoughts, what will they do if they realize that I am going to kill them?*

Matt figured that it wasn't just others who could be in danger. He too was at risk.

I have to control my emotions, he thought. *I can't let them know what I intend to do. And I can't think bad thoughts of others, either.*

Matt sat on the front step of his house and tried to calm down. He had to be cold and distant. After a bit, he slowly turned the knob on his front door and snuck back into his house.

Quietly, he crept up the stairs and into his bedroom. There, he crawled into bed and waited for his ants to return.

In the morning, he would buy one last packet of candy. The ants were uncontrollable without the Pop Rocks, and he knew he couldn't keep them sedated with the candy forever. He would have to put them to sleep—permanently.

ANT FARM

Chapter 28

Matt awoke the next morning with a start. He hadn't heard the ants return during the night and wasn't sure if in fact they had.

He stepped carefully over to the closet and listened for activity. He had to know if they were in there. Slowly, he lifted the lid of the chest.

Inside, the ants slept, piled on top of each other. Matt quietly shut the lid and backed out of the closet.

Being careful not to awaken the ants, Matt got dressed and ready for school, although school was not where he was heading. He couldn't take the chance of the ants hurting anyone else while he sat in class all day.

Today, he would skip school and make a visit to the corner store.

Matt tried to act normally. He had breakfast with his family and packed up his backpack. He didn't want his parents or his ants to know what he was up to.

As the school bell rang, signaling the start of classes, Matt sat on a tree trunk in the woods, waiting for the store to open.

At nine o'clock exactly, Matt went into the store, the bells clanging against the glass door.

"Good morning, Matthew. Aren't you supposed to be in school now?" said Mr. Stoops.

He was unpacking several boxes and restocking the shelves.

"There's some problem at the school. We're off for the rest of the day," Matt answered.

"Lucky you," said Mr. Stoops. "Well, enjoy your day off, young fella."

Matt went over to the candy rack, and only then did he realize he had another problem. He only had thirty cents in his pocket. He also knew his piggy bank was wiped clean.

He needed the candy. It was a matter of public safety.

Maybe I could ask Mr. Stoops to lend me a pack and I could pay him tomorrow, he thought. *Nah, that wouldn't work. What do I tell him...that I'm protecting*

*the town from giant ants? Plus, I couldn't pay him
tomorrow, either.*

Matt was scared. He had to get rid of the ants.
He didn't know what would happen next.

*I'll have to just take a pack. It's just one
pack...and I'll pay Mr. Stoops back as soon as I can. I'll
leave the money on the floor sometime. He'll never
know.*

He looked around nervously and then quickly
grabbed a pack and stuffed it in his pocket. His heart
was pounding in his throat, and his face was blood red.

He tried to act calm, but his feet walked much
quicker than he wanted them to. He left the store in a
matter of seconds.

He made it! He felt ashamed at first. But he
managed to convince himself that the safety of
everyone in the area was more important than a pack of
candy.

Within a few minutes, Matt arrived home. The
problem was that no one else was home and the doors
were all locked. He checked around the entire house.

He had to get in. He looked up and saw the
damage the ants had done to the back of the house.
Seeing the hole, which matched exactly with the one at
Jack's house and the one at school, reminded him of the
danger inside.

Under the deck, he found an old crowbar and
decided to try to pry open the basement door. He put

the crowbar into the crack of the door and leaned on it with all of his weight.

His hand slipped off and smashed through one of the window panes of the door. There was a fairly large cut on his arm, but overall it didn't hurt that much.

Through the opening, he was able to reach inside and unlock the sliding bolt on the door. It wasn't exactly how he intended to do it, but it did get the job done.

Matt knew his parents were going to be upset with him, but he needed to destroy the ants before they got out again. As he entered the basement, he noticed an old metal trash can in the corner, and an idea came to him.

He knew he was going to have a hard time destroying the ants. Not only were they dangerous, but he also wasn't sure if he would have the nerve to kill things that he had considered pets. He figured he could just put them in the metal trash can, where they couldn't escape, and let them die on their own.

He grabbed the trash can and headed upstairs. At the bottom of the basement steps, he saw a can of bug spray. He tossed it into the trash can and continued up the stairs.

He had to finish the job before his parents came home. How else could he explain what he was doing with an old metal trash can in his room?

With no time to spare, he set the can on the floor by his bedroom closet. He took out the can of bug spray and set it on his dresser. Then he reached in his pocket for the stolen Pop Rocks.

As soon as he opened the closet door, the scratching began. Matt opened the lid, and they all began to beg in unison.

The herd of ants followed him as he led them over to the trash can. He ripped open the packet of candy and poured it into the can, causing a huge racket.

Moments later, the ants were eating in the bottom of the trash can, and the lid was put tightly in place. After they ate and were calm, he would use the entire can of bug spray to put them to rest.

The sound of the ants' wrestling for the Pop Rocks was deafening against the metal can. Matt was worried that his parents would hear it if they came home.

"Come on, hurry up and finish already," he pleaded.

Finally, the feeding frenzy ceased. They had all settled down. There was no movement. He had to do it now.

He picked up the can of bug spray and put his hand on the lid of the trash can. With a deep breath to gather his courage, he lifted the lid.

At that moment, Matt heard the front door open and close loudly.

"Matthew? Are you in here?" his dad said in a loud and what sounded like angry voice.

Matt put the lid down and ran out of his room, closing the door behind him.

"Yeah, Dad, I'm upstairs," he answered, his voice quivering.

His father came up the steps and met him in the hallway.

"I just got a call from Mr. Stoops down at the corner store! Do you have something you want to say to me?"

"Uh...Dad...you don't understand. I had to..."

"You had to what? You mean to tell me that you had to steal candy! AND WHY AREN'T YOU IN SCHOOL?" Matt had never seen his father so angry. His face was red, and his eyes were bulging.

Then Matt heard the sounds of movement coming from inside the trash can.

"Answer me!" his father said, grabbing Matt's arm.

"Dad, please, I'm sorry. I'll pay it back. Just don't be upset with me. It's really important. Please stop yelling!"

He could hear the ants banging against the trash can in his room. They were getting angry.

"How could I not be upset with you? You know stealing is wrong!"

The pounding against the metal was ferocious now.

"And what are you doing to make all that noise in there?" he demanded.

"Dad, you have to get out of here. You don't understand!" Matt pleaded. He grabbed his father's hand, urging him to move away.

"You're darn right I don't understand!" he said as he walked down the hall towards Matt's room.

Just then Matt heard the trash can tip over with a loud *CLANG!* He could hear the metal lid roll to a stop on the floor.

"Dad, seriously, get out of here!" Matt screamed.

He pushed past his dad and stepped in front of him. Matt could hear the ants on the other side of the wall, their massive, angry feet pounding on the ground like a herd of elephants.

Matt's father stopped in his tracks, trying to figure out what kind of animal was in the room.

The pounding thunder had now turned into frantic scratching and clawing. Matt knew that the wall would not stop them. They could rip through the material like a human could bite into an apple.

"Dad! Run! I can't control them!"

"Matt, what's making that noise?" his father demanded. "You need to tell me what's going on!"

"There's no time. Can't you hear them? They're coming! You've made them angry, and they're going to kill you!"

"I don't know what kind of game you're playing, but it's not..."

Then he saw the paint on the wall splintering and the plaster start to crumble. The hole increased in size at an amazing rate as the white wall was being consumed by masses of black death.

Seconds later, they had broken through, and they were hungry.

ANT FARM

Chapter 29

"Go, Dad! Run!"

Matt's dad staggered against the wall. The closest ant lurched forward and drove its mandibles into his ankle. He kicked violently, flailing his arms and legs until the ant was thrown off, smacking against the wall. The ant bolted back at him the instant it had landed on the floor.

By this time, the other ants were crawling on his legs, trying to find an open space to inject their poisonous stingers into their prey.

"STOP IT! STOP IT! I COMMAND YOU TO STOP!" Matt yelled.

There were other ants now, tugging at his dad's legs, ripping his jeans to shreds as a human would tear tissue paper.

"MATT! GET THEM OFF!" his dad wailed. Chunks of flesh were being ripped from his legs.

Matt looked up and, seeing his father half-covered with the monsters, let go of the two ants he was trying to hold back. He knew that he could not control them without more Pop Rocks. He ran into his room to where the trash can had tipped over, searching for any remains of the candy.

There, in the bottom, a few of the uneaten pieces were left. Matt desperately snatched them and ran back to the hallway.

"Here ya go, guys! Come on, want a treat?" he pleaded. By now, his father was a cloud of black and red, mandibles biting and ripping faster than before.

Matt waved the Pop Rocks over the pile so they could smell the treat. One by one, the ants turned their attention towards him. As they crawled off of the banquet to join the line of hungry followers, Matt saw his father lying in a heap of blood, torn fabric, and other liquids.

"Get up, Dad. You can do it." *Oh, please let this work*, he thought.

Matt led the pack of begging ants back to the trash can, picked it up, and tossed the Pop Rocks into it. The ants frantically followed the rattling of the hard candies bouncing on the bottom of the can as they climbed up the side with ease. This time, Matt had the bug spray ready.

"All right, boys, this is your last meal."

Matt held the lid in his left hand and began spraying the poison with his right. At first, the ants ignored the deadly gas as they fought each other for the few remaining bits of candy. But soon, the candy was gone, and the ants became aware that they were being attacked themselves.

They struggled to climb up the sides of the can to save themselves and to finish off their leftover prey in the hallway. Matt emptied the bug spray and pushed the lid down as tightly as possible, just before the ants were able to reach the top. Several of the creatures' legs stuck out of the lid like branches of a dead tree. Matt leaned with all of his might on the lid, but the strength of the ants was becoming too much for him.

The ants were no longer trying to protect Matt; they were trying to save themselves. With a sudden thrust, the lid was forced off, and one of the ants' powerful jaws snapped shut on Matt's arm. Matt yelped in pain and let go of the lid just as his father stumbled over and fell on top of the trash can. The force of his adult body slammed the lid closed again, severing the head of the ant that bit into Matt's arm. The mandibles released, and the head of the ant fell to the floor. Blood squirted from its neck while its jaws kept biting.

Matt and his dad held the lid down while the ants gasped their last breaths. They pounded on the sides of the can, hoping to break free, but the trap held firm. A minute later, the noise had stopped.

Matt looked over at his dad, whose clothes were torn to shreds. He lay over the top of the can because his legs were so badly bitten.

"Dad, you made it," Matt said in disbelief. "I'm so sorry, it's all my fault."

"Are you kidding me?" he said, wincing in pain. "You saved me." He looked down at the decapitated head lying motionless of the floor. "So what the heck are these things, anyway?"

"Let's get you cleaned up, and then I'll explain everything."

He ran to find a chair for his father and helped him to the seat. After fetching first aid supplies, Matt thought about how he should begin. Putting drops of alcohol on cotton balls, he told his dad about the first day the ants had arrived. He talked about the ants' odd behavior when they were given Pop Rocks and how the creatures began to crave the candy.

As Matt began to clean his father's wounds, he explained how the ants grew bigger and stronger every day and eventually were moved into his closet. Matt paused, and tried to think of how to relate this last part—why the ants had tried to kill his dad. He picked up the bandages and began wrapping, telling the story with as much detail as possible...

* * *

"So it's my fault that two people are dead...and I almost got you killed."

"How could you have known?" his dad reasoned. "Sure, you shouldn't have hid the ants from your mother and me, but you acted as soon as you understood the problem."

Both sat in silence for a moment, Matt overwhelmed with his mistakes and his father not believing what he had just experienced.

"So what do we do now?" asked Matt. "Should we tell Mom?"

"Of course, we have to. You always need to tell the truth, even if it is something crazy like this. But first, we have to clean this place up before she gets home. If your mother sees one of these monsters, she'll have a heart attack."

Together, they dragged the heavy trash can down the stairs and into the woods behind their house. It took an hour to dig a hole that was deep enough to hold all of them, and by the end, what little strength they once had was gone. Matt lifted the lid on the can and looked at the grotesque, lifeless pile of ants.

The two of them leaned against the trash can, tipping it onto its side. The ants spilled out into the deep hole, their hard bodies landing on each other with a sickening sound. Ten minutes later, the hole was filled with dirt.

After it was finally finished, Matt's dad smiled at him and shook his head. "What a day, huh?"

He put his arm on Matt's shoulder, and Matt helped him hobble back to the house. They collapsed on the two couches in the living room and waited to tell their incredible story. Matt was happy that they had worked together to solve a problem. He had saved his dad's life and possibly the entire neighborhood.

* * *

That night, deep beneath the ground, a large ant woke from a long, dazed nap. His leg twitched as he regained consciousness. Soon all of his legs were moving, and his jaws chewed easily through the soil as he began to dig.

Get ready for the next spine-chilling tale coming from Screamin Calhoun...

THE GRAVES

Visit Tombstonesbooks.com for more...

Made in USA - Kendallville, IN
1187618_9781532956898
12.14.2020 1653